Zobha
Stories From India

Series 1

Ukiyoto Publishing

All global publishing rights are held by

Ukiyoto Publishing

Published in 2019

Content Copyright © **Ukiyoto**

ISBN 9789364945912

All rights reserved.
No part of this publication may be reproduced, transmitted, or stored in a retrieval system, in any form by any means, electronic, mechanical, photocopying, recording or otherwise, without the prior permission of the publisher.

The moral right of the author has been asserted.

This is a work of fiction. Names, characters, businesses, places, events, locales, and incidents are either the products of the author's imagination or used in a fictitious manner. Any resemblance to actual persons, living or dead, or actual events is purely coincidental.

This book is sold subject to the condition that it shall not by way of trade or otherwise, be lent, resold, hired out or otherwise circulated, without the publisher's prior consent, in any form of binding or cover other than that in which it is published.

Zobha represents Brightness, the festival of lights finding its roots in India

This title holds in its pages the very essence of India, its people and its culture, conveyed through a selection of short stories by few of the best authors of India.

CONTENTS

Elephant's Teeth *By Sana Shanawaz*	1
The Unsettled Peace *By Olivi Roy Chowdhury*	7
The Unwanted Sibling *By Anju Chandna*	14
The Metaphor of Memories *By Abhidip Ray*	22
About the Authors	*43*

Elephant's Teeth

by Sana Shanawaz

"Now it's more delicious and nutritious," said Zubeda, handling a glass of saffron milk to Aafreen. She smiled, and Zubeda smiled back.

"Such a kind woman. I'm more than lucky to have her as my mother-in-law", Aafreen thought, sipping the milk, while resting on a sofa, gently caressing her baby bump.

Zubeda was a dusky woman with black eyes and a short and slim body always neatly dressed in a cotton saree. The smell of her biryani had gotten her many friends from the neighborhood ever since she moved to Barkatpura street, years back. "Zubeda apa has magic in her hands." They would say.

Though her aching joints had made all the smell of kitchen condiments a thing of past, she was confident she would never forget the recipe of biryani. A baby shower was going to held at her house that day. All her excuses had gone for a walk, the moment she realized she was going to be a granny soon. Once again she took charge of the kitchen.

Aafreen entered the kitchen with the empty glass in hand while she was searching for utensils. She tried to help her, straining her back, bending low.

"*Nakko, nakko-* No, no. You go and get ready for the *dawat-* party. *Log aate hi honge-* Guests can arrive anytime.", Zubeda protested. Aafreen insisted for one more minute, then went back, thoughtful.

Zubeda liked Aafreen, she was beautiful. "She is the perfect match for our Nayeem," Shameem had said when they first met her. She wasn't fond of Shameem much, her habit of poking nose in her family matters, her long visits and constant demands for kaddu ki kheer was enough to make it worse. "*Mere Bhai ka Ghar Matlab Mera Ghar* - My brother's family-my family." she would defend. But, people always listen or try to impress the ones they don't like. She had fixed the marriage on the spot, and she never regretted it.

Both her children were beautiful, her daughter, Nadia inherited a blunt nose from her aunt, but her fair skin made it less noticeable. Nayeem was handsome too. She was glad they inherited the major element of beauty - fair complexion (at least for the majority of people in the locality) from their father.

As she took the onions to slice, her mind wandered through the walls of her classroom when she was but a kid. She had an elder sister, Shireen, who was as white as milk and all her schoolmates opened their mouths in awe when their relationship was disclosed. Once their physical education teacher remarked, in front of her whole class, "*Ek doodh hai to doosri chai-* One is like the milk and the other like tea."

She remembered stiffening in her seat, and the words penetrated deep in her ears and had pricked her eyes. A thick sheet of tears came out of her eyes, she quickly bent her head low to hide them. A chorus of laughter had filled the room, some unknowingly, some followed hesitatingly. Later, they picked up a nickname for her "*Chai, chai* - Tea, tea," they used to tease her in assembly, during lunch hours and even in front of Mukheet sir, her favorite Teacher.

She heard somewhere that saffron is good for the skin, and it works wonders if combined with milk. She can never bear her children to go through the same sufferings as her. So she made sure that Aafreen drink that every day. Though, she didn't reveal the purpose behind it.

Aafreen looked pretty in a pink-colored Kaftan kurta which came down to her knees, paired with cream-colored palazzo pants. She took her scarf over her head which made her hair less visible. A long-thick jasmine garland dotted with red roses hung across her neck, her face glowed pink.

"Is it the magic of the coming baby or the arrival of Nayeem?", someone in the crowd teased. She flushed, her cheeks showcased many colors of pinkish-red.

"Zubeda apa has got a beautiful bride," said the lady who was constantly apologizing to Zubeda for not attending her son's marriage. Zubeda smiled back at her compliment, nodding, a strange feeling of pride occupied her. She felt safe.

"Come, come. Everyone. Here, to the *Dastarkhwaan*." Shameem said taking charge of the whole dawat. Zubeda looked bemused, but she managed to smile.

2 Months later

One early morning, Aafreen sat on the sofa in the living room, her arms wrapped around a small baby girl. She was looking less presentable, the baby didn't let her spare a minute to wash her face. Though, it had rarely affected her shiny, flawless face. She had to manage all the chores. The overwhelming care by her mother-in-law was a distant dream now. She didn't even give a single affectionate glance at the girl. At first, she thought because it's a girl. But, no. It was something strange and weird she couldn't understand.

Zubeda was cleaning the rice, spread in a large stainless steel plate when the doorbell rang. Before she could rush to open it, it was pushed open by a stout, tall, fair-looking woman with a reddish-pink stain on her lips. She walked inside, chewing paan.

"Welcome, Shameem apa." blurted Zubeda, half-surprised, half-scared.

"It's my brother's house, I can come anytime here. If he had lived today, he would have cheerfully informed me about his granddaughter." She tilted her mouth sideways to express anger and displeasure and headed towards Aafreen.

She asked in her typical Hyderabadi language, a combination of Hindi, Telugu, and Urdu. "*Kya naam rakha hai? Vo to bhi bolsakte nai?*" - "What's her name? Can it be revealed, at least?"

Zubeda tried to answer, "We were about to tell you. It happened so early that....

"Early? She's two weeks old, right?" Shameem frowned. "Anyways, leave it."

She gave a red signal to the argument and took hold of the baby, "Name?" She asked, raising an eyebrow.

Aafreen got so fascinated by this drama that she almost forgot answering her.

"N-Nasiya Aunty"

"Nasiya Aunty? Is that her name?"

"No, I mean, she is Nasiya."

"*Accha, accha* - Okay, okay." She laughed aloud, patting Aafreen's thigh, almost hurting her.

Aafreen looked slightly irritated but managed to smile.

"*Ale le... tutu tu..*" Aunty started cooing her.

"Doesn't she look like Nadia, her nose and eyes too. I bet her forehead is exactly the same. You know Nadia? Your aunt."

"But she's a fair skin- umm.." The words escaped Zubeda's mouth and regretted the moment it came out.

Aafreen stiffened in her sofa, it felt like something hammered inside her heart. All the strange behavior of Zubeda made sense to her. She got up angrily and took the baby from Shameem. "She needs to be fed, Aunty.", she made an excuse and left the room.

Something ached inside Zubeda. She couldn't help the way she felt. Hadn't she disliked this kind of behavior all her life? Didn't she think of eliminating such hatred all her life?

Maybe she's found eliminating much easier than accepting.

The Unsettled Peace

by Olivi Roy Chouwdhury

They say it is better to have loved and lost than to not have loved at all. Ryan had heard this somewhere but could not quite remember where. It was a phrase which he very well understood because he had experienced it all.

As he sat down pondering, he questioned himself "Why me? Why has it always had to be me?"

Riddhi and Ryan went to the same college. Riddhi was a simple girl and she did not have a social life like most of her college mates. To her, college life meant studying and proving to her parents that she could be the one who not only excelled in academics but also was equally able to win any beauty contest by keeping a check on her grooming skills.

Riddhi thought she did not fit into either of the category and was quite ashamed of herself. She did not value herself enough.

Grooming herself to become a beauty queen just for pleasing someone else was not something she was ready to do. She opted for the second one and decided to study hard so that she could at least get some decent marks and make her parents proud.

Her parents were very understanding and it was something she wanted to prove to them, but mostly to herself.

Riddhi was overwhelmed when Ryan proposed to her just the way she had imagined in her dreams.

Bending on one knee with a ring in his hand, he told her "You know that I love you right? Will you marry me?".

It was clichéd but to Riddhi nothing mattered more than saying, "Yes, yes of course I will". Tears of joy rolled down her cheeks as he put the ring on. She was surprised to find that the ring fit perfectly into her finger. They had been dating for quite some time now. She was overjoyed because she was engaged to the man of her dreams.

Then came the most difficult phase of breaking this news to both the families.

Riddhi and Ryan tried their level best in making their parents understand why they were perfect for each other. A marriage in the Indian society factors in the two families coming together as well along with the couple.

For desi parents, arranged marriage is a more pragmatic option. According to them, love matters in a relationship, but it is not the only thing that makes a marriage successful.

Riddhi had read somewhere that a perfect marriage is about two imperfect people sharing a life and embracing each other the way they are. Whether it is love or arranged marriage, every couple needs to accept their differences, be persistent, love each other beyond boundaries on both good and bad days. But then again, a love marriage is not a cake walk either. It comes with its own set of challenges. She truly believed that and was ready to face it with the love of her life.

After lots of struggle, days of coaxing and anxious nights finally came the day when both families agreed to have a meeting. Riddhi was tensed about the outcome of the meeting.

Ryan comforted her by saying that everything will be alright and that very soon they will be together for ever. Riddhi almost had a panic attack as she waited patiently in her room awaiting the result of the meeting of both the families, which would decide their fate.

Just as she was about to call Ryan and ask about the meeting, a message from Ryan popped up on her screen. She opened it anxiously and as soon as she read the message her lips parted into a broad smile and she was overjoyed. She felt so relieved that she jumped madly on her bed. All had gone well, and the auspicious day was set.

Then started the never-ending long list of chores including meeting a bridal consultant, fixing the wedding venue, rehearsal dinners, trousseau shopping, confirming and re-confirming delivery times, preparing the guest list and so on. All seemed to happen in a flash. Riddhi started feeling like a Disney princess ready for the dream wedding she always wished for. She promised herself that once all the madness of the event is over, she would be living her anticipated happily ever after. (Or would she?)

Soon came the big day. Riddhi felt intoxicated in happiness and everything happened in a blur. She was decked up like a doll, all religious ceremonies whizzed by. The only emotion she felt throughout the process was nervousness and everything felt unreal. Was it really happening?

At one moment she was smiling, and the next she was crying holding her parents during the "Vidaai" ceremony. This moment was the toughest of all for her. Having to leave her parents was not an easy task. She had been preparing herself for this moment, but all those preparations went in vain. The emotional turmoil was too much for her to handle.

She was welcomed by her in-laws in the perfect traditional way and it exceeded her expectations. She was stuffed with sweets, showered with gifts and happiness. Holding her husband's hand, they were ready to enter her new life. Calling him her "husband" felt unreal. She was nervous. She did not know what to expect, more so what was expected from her. But as time passed by everything seemed to fall in place and she tried her level best to be the perfect Indian daughter in law.

Soon it was almost a year. Managing household chores and office at the same time began to take a toll on her. However hard she tried, she was unable to balance both her personal and professional life. Soon started the fights, days of no talking, endless lectures and disagreements.

Riddhi started getting frustrated and depressed and so did Ryan. But still both tried to cooperate with each other as much as possible.

It was 1st July, when both Ryan and Riddhi had an ugly fight. Both blamed each other ruthlessly. As they say, 'Sometimes we need to be brave enough to be imperfect with someone'. Riddhi had already gotten ready for office. She had an important presentation that day with the client. If all went well, she would get a promotion which she was already worthy of and had been waiting for a long time. The fight had really shaken Riddhi from inside. She was unable to concentrate on anything. With shaking hands, she took the car keys, wiped away a tear that trickled down her cheek and was about to leave for office.

Ryan called her from behind and said that they both should not go to office that day. He advised they should rather sit down and sort out the matters that had been driving them apart for the past few months.

Riddhi turned back, a little relieved, and with a small smile on her lips said that all will be fine if they both are together. She hugged him and said that she had a very important presentation that day. She promised him that as soon as she is done with it she will come running home to his arms.

She hugged him tight again and whispered into his ears, "Wish me luck!"

Ryan wished her all the luck in the world, and she left home with a smile on her face. She was determined that things would change for the better and everything would be alright.

It was 10:15am when Ryan's phone rang. He was just about to leave for office so that he could come back home to his beloved like they promised to each other. Seeing an unknown number pop up on his phone screen, he frowned and picked up the call. A rather serious voice on the other side rendered his entire world to come crashing down. He felt nauseated. He wanted to delay the moment of truth for as long as he could. "This is not true. It can't be happening" he kept muttering to himself. He felt like he was going to pass out. His worst fear of losing his beloved had just come true.

Riddhi had met with an accident and there were no survivors. It was a head on collision with a truck. Her face was completely disfigured. The cops had found her phone and were able to trace it back to Ryan.

If only Riddhi had listened to him and stayed back. The last message she was still typing to him was "I love you and I will make everything right. Just be there for me as I need you. Love you always and forever".

The Unwanted Sibling

by Anju Chandna

Anamika paces up and down the corridor of her office waiting for her cell phone to ring, her heeled shoes making a rhythmic clicking sound. The flight was scheduled to land at 11:00 am in New Delhi and it was already time. Finally, her cell phone rings. 'Hello!' The soft female voice on the other end of the line instantly erases the creases on Anamika's brow as she raises her voice in response.

'Didi, can you hear me? I've landed and am on my way home'. Hi Mohini, where are you?' Anamika catches the growing lump in her throat, steading the quiver in her voice 'I'm on my way home too. I'll quickly pick my things and see you at home!'. Anamika grabs her handbag and runs down the flight of stairs. Throwing her things in the back of the car she quickly gets behind the wheel. The road looks deserted in the scorching summer sun, Anamika's mind wanders to that fateful day when Mohini was born.

Mohini was fifteen years younger to her, the youngest of the three siblings with Anamika being the eldest, followed by Sujata. A star performer in school and the university, Mohini was returning home after completing her graduation from a prestigious university in Australia. Mohini, endearingly called Moni was the 'little angel' of the household. Her birth at the ripe age of her parents was not an accident, it was a pre-meditated effort to have an heir for the family. No ritual which could possibly convert an X-chromosome into a Y was spared by her grandmother, including consultation with priests and astrologers about the exact date and month of conception by Anamika's mother. Anamika was a mute spectator in this evolving family drama all around her. She was almost fifteen, on the brink of womanhood herself and mature enough to decipher the hushed tones her parents used to discuss the arrival of their 'son'.

Early morning one day Anamika woke up to some commotion in the house. 'So, this is the day they've been waiting for', she thought to herself. Her mother had been hospitalized early that morning after complaining of pain she learnt and she was to escort her younger sibling to school. School seemed especially long that day, Anamika was quiet and withdrawn waiting with confused anticipation of what was about to come. She could obviously not tell her teenage friends that her mother was having a baby and become a laughing stock of her school. The ride back from school must have lasted a decade that afternoon, 'Why is it taking so unusually long to reach home?' 'Will mother survive this ordeal?' 'Will her family actually get the baby boy they so desperately desire?' 'What if it's a girl?' Her adolescent mind had questions aplenty, but no answers. The school bus came to a halt as she saw her father waiting for her and Sujata at the bus stop. 'We have to go to the hospital' her father said in a flat expressionless tone. 'What is it, papa?' The baby? 'You'll soon get to see it!' he said nonchalantly.

Anamika reluctantly followed him to the car, holding on to Sujata's hand tightly, as if out of reassurance. They reached the end of the staircase leading to the first-floor hospital room where her mother was admitted. Anamika's grandmother was sitting on the bench with two elderly women near the rails of the staircase. Sujata ran to greet her grandma, she lifted the little girl and put her on her lap and then turned to Anamika. 'Anu, do you want to see your new sister?', she said, darting a vexed glance at her father. 'What had father done to earn grandma's wrath?', thought Anamika and turned around to look at her father. This was not the man she'd left at home that very morning. The man who sat there instead with shoulders hunched from some invisible burden was a figure of utter dejection, a man whose dream of an heir, of an unborn entity who could open the doors of salvation for him had been shattered. Anamika was aghast. Fifteen years of upbringing in a loving household stood juxtaposed to this fleeting moment of revelation for her.

Her father nudged her to follow him into the hospital room where her mother lay. Sujata rushed to her mother and hugged her, Anamika stood frozen, refusing to look into the older woman's eyes. She felt a strange mix of emotions for her mother, hatred, betrayal, pity even. 'Why did she have to shatter the normalcy of her life?', she thought to herself. Still preoccupied in her thoughts, her gaze was drawn to the small bundle of pink flesh lying by her mother's side. She moved closer to the bed and gently pulled away the cloth to see the baby's face. Oh! The most beautiful pair of eyes stared back at her. Anamika quickly looked away. 'How could she let her mind be overpowered by this innocent creature when her whole being was rebelling against the very reason of its creation?'

Three days later mother came back home. Home was never the same. There were visitors who ostensibly came to bless the young one. The underlying agenda of the visit, however, was to bestow their worldly wisdom about bringing up three girls in such dangerous and vicious times, the pitfalls of having to deal with such a huge age gap between siblings and on and on and on it went, much to Anamika's chagrin. Father put up a stoic front, mother was quiet while grandmother was happy to lament about how destiny had played a vicious trick on them. And then one day the visits stopped. Anamika took a sigh of relief as some semblance of sanity returned and the business of getting around life resumed.

School time in the morning, study time in the afternoon and some play time later. Everything was back to normal. Except that now there was a new member in the family eagerly awaiting Anamika's return. As the summer gave way to winter, Anamika came to be greeted more and more by her kid sister every day when she came back from school in the afternoon. Moni would invariably be perched on the railing of the balcony, her eyes eagerly waiting for her siblings to return and the daily ritual of climbing the staircase became the 'highpoint' of the day. Moni would crawl towards the top of the staircase and on seeing Anamika and Sujata, would burst into shrieks of joy. Her gurgling sound would ring in the entire household.

One day as Anamika set foot on the spiral staircase leading to their first-floor apartment, she saw Moni precariously dangling from the edge of the last step, oblivious to the danger of falling over. Throwing her bag aside, Anamika swung to her side and leaped to catch her baby sister in time. Thrown off guard by the sudden commotion, Moni started howling. Cuddling and soothing the baby, Anamika walked in and put it on the floor. Sujata ran inside gushing 'Mom, didi saved Moni today'. What followed was a detailed account of the baby's imminent fall and her timely rescue by Anamika. Mother looked up and gave Anamika a quizzical look, 'She could've fallen from the stairs, why can't you look after her?', said Anamika, glaring at her mother, her estrangement with the latter writ large on her face.

Moni was growing and so was Anamika's attention towards her. Moni was the first one to wake up every morning, her wake up wailings would create an instant flutter in the household. Father would run to fetch her milk bottle and mother would get busy with the unending errands that a little baby can generate. But Moni had eyes only for her siblings. She would sneak out of her bed, crawl to the bed pole for support and somehow manage to reach where her siblings slept. With her little fingers, she would reach out to their faces and play with their eyes, ears and nose. Anamika always tried hard to push her hand out of the way. But the little hand was persistent. After much persuasion, it finally found its mate. Anamika would make mocking snoring sounds and would bite the little finger only to send Moni into ripples of laughter.

One day as Anamika came back from school she saw an unfamiliar car parked in front of their house. Sensing visitors, she cautiously entered the living room. She was met with strangers, a lady and a man appearing to be her husband. 'What's going on?" she enquired from her mother. Avoiding her gaze, mother nudged her out of the living room and quietly replied 'They are some distant relatives from your father's side, they heard about Moni and so they came.' Anamika took a breath waiting for her mother to finish but when no words followed, ... 'So?' she asked. 'What do they want?' 'They live in the US and have been married for many years but have no child, so they want to take Moni' she said in an expressionless tone. 'Take away! What do you mean take away?', yelled Anamika. 'Moni is not a burger and this is not a take-away joint' she retorted, her eyes beginning to swell up with tears. Mother looked at her trying to read the expression on her face. 'But I thought you don't like the baby, you've been so angry....you have stopped talking to me and your father, Anu....we thought it was best for all of us....they are good people known to our family....Moni will be pampered, she'll go to the US with them....they have money and a good house....' it went on and on, mother was muttering but Anamika had started to get up. She stormed into the bedroom where Moni was playing, picked her up and came back to where mother was standing. 'I am not giving her to anyone, she belongs to us' retorted Anamika, the words literally dropping from her mouth, surprising even herself and loud enough for everyone sitting in the adjoining room to hear.

The 'distant relatives' apparently overheard the remark and quietly left. Anamika walked into the living room with her little sibling perched on her arm, father looked perplexed. 'We thought this was best for all of our family' ..... his voice trailed off with a gradual sense of relief creeping in.

Anamika's thoughts are interrupted by the sight of a pretty young lady standing in front of her car bonnet as she approaches her house. Wiping her tears away, she gets down from the car. The two women give a long loving look to each other, 'It's good to see you, Sis'! as the two women run towards each other to wind up in a warm embrace while everyone in the family looks on.

'My best Didi', remarks Moni teasingly. 'And you are my savior, my kid sister! It is you who taught me unconditional love and forgiveness' remarks Anamika.

The Metaphor of Memories

by Abhidip Ray

I

"Bed number 42, bed number 42…"

The distant call of the attendant from Emergency sounded unclear from this side of the glass – it's the smoking zone. Anuj has just lit up his second consecutive stick of Gold Flake lights when the call came in. For a moment, it didn't make any difference to his unheeding subconscious. Then steadily, as it continued to strike his numb eardrums, Anuj realized; the last few hours have given his wife Shreya a new identity: Bed no. 42!

Everything was supposed to turn out okay; at least that's how Anuj had imagined his life thus far. And if truth be told, he has been steady in his path, in the travel towards a destination planned by his own. He's 32 now, lead consultant at Bates Chi, happily married and a to-be father, also trying to co-partner a bakery Café library with Shreya. And with his parents staying back at Durgapur, they are the monarchs of their own empire.

Anuj was in the process of booking the cab for their final doctor's visit before admission and Shreya was climbing down the stairs, one by one. She had one hand on her swollen impregnated belly and the other on the cemented stair railings. Anuj's parents are all set to arrive the day after for assisting them through this phase. The quiet November afternoon at 76 Dover Lane had nothing exceptional to mention, to indicate the sudden to-be turn of their lives into a raging hurricane. She's eight months due and the expected date for delivery was set at around 25th of December – the coming of a Jesus.

And then, out of the blue everything happened in a blur. The driver's call sounded sharp and out of place within the tranquil quietude, and amidst that sudden cacophony, Shreya's cautious feet missed a step. She was still only halfway down and the other half she came down rolling. Anuj stood shocked; too slow to respond as the neurons in his brain transmitted pulses slower than time. He rushed, but it was too late. Shreya's head had hit the walls in the corner, rendering her unconscious. The white marbles on the floor had traces of carmine blood all over and in one glimpse, reality snatched away all those lucid dreams and strategic plans. Anuj's eyes searched through the contacts on his phone as the nameless names got blurred soon enough with the impending tears and its haze. It was a juncture of utter confusion - he hesitated to leave her alone, yet the need to arrange a correction overwhelmed his thoughts. The next few hours passed in a complete daze as Anuj held a brittle love onto his lap. Waves of tears broke all barricades of decency as he rushed through the insurance papers on the ambulance seats.

Back here at the nursing home, a host of specialist doctors surrounded Shreya on arrival. They checked her history of ailments and went through her scrolls of prescriptions. Anuj stood there all the time, his nervous breaths hushed as droplets of sweat came down his forehead.

Is this how one feels like being at the center of a tornado? - All helpless with nothing to see, apart from a faint mirage of light at the end of the tunnel. The birds among the high trees still chirp though, and butterflies still flutter their blue wings, yet their stories are nothing but folklores at the times of Hope.

The attendants changed Shreya's robes and gave her the necessary medications behind the while veiled curtains. Anuj decided to take a break across within the glasses of smoke. Outside the walls, in the middle of the grey sky, an eagle flew high, her wings spread out wide as she cut through the air circling amidst the clouds. Somehow for reasons unknown, Anuj gets lost always looking at the sky and its chained birds. The hour of decision is looming over and with every passing second, he visualized the golden phoenix flying a little further away. And then the dream broke as his dead senses got revived with the mundane call of the attendant – "Bed number 42".

"She needs to be operated immediately", the doctor informed a rushing Anuj, "there are some formalities to be done, I have informed the service desk, please fill those up while we make the OT ready", then with a pause, he added – "She had quite a few internal hemorrhages and concussions, it's serious".

Anuj's voice choked. The surgeon seemed someone stern, with age approximately within the high forties, he in his deep jade robes and round glasses, demanded respect. Yet with the word 'Operation' there came in another set of fears which Anuj had tried to push away till now, the bunch of questions whose answers he feared to know; yet those which needs to be asked. Sparing a small sigh for himself, Anuj adjusted the roughness in his voice. The lump at the center of his chest started weighing a galaxy as he came to ask the dreaded question.

"Doctor, what about the baby? Is it safe?"

For a moment the doc hesitated. Then taking a deep breath within, he spoke in a voice perhaps to soften the wounds and deliver a faraway hope – "It's too early to ask Mr. Sen", then in a tone slightly more comfortable, slightly more reassuring - "There may come a time we need to decide, be ready please..."

II

It seemed like a memory of another time, a memory of a thousand Springs back, when their love grew like dancing Orchids in the Alps, when it held designs of fallen maple on a freshly brewed mug of Cappuccino, when all her griefs and anguishes could be bribed, when 'Future' and 'Family' were still concepts of a far-flung wonderland. But as they all say, time runs at a pace faster than our sentience can detect and on following the trails of the departed calendars, the date of this memoir just run half a decade back!

It was a windy wet evening of July. Anuj had just returned from his workshop in Paris and the duo was to meet about a month after. Their recent segregation had caused instances of passionate huffs on both sides of the aisle and seeing each other in-person became a necessity for their own sake.

Shreya stood, waiting; even on that day. A few last-minute household chores coupled with the meagre availability of public transport in the drizzle made things tough for Anuj as he stepped down at Golpark bus stand around thirty minutes late - it was a drenched falling dusk in a nostalgic city. The shiny wet crows searched for a viable shelter, as the corner of Anuj's eyes caught the shadows of Shreya. There she was in that Bohemian kurta – the blue and beige strips wandered all over its cotton fibers without a set rhythm or pattern, yet the disjoint chaos overall replicated an idyllic architecture. He moved towards her; there was a magic in the instant and the hour of being together after almost an eternity, gave Anuj the déjà vu to that oblivion. The random techno beats ended as a melancholic Bryan Adams sung into his ears from within the queue:

"Look into my eyes; you'll see what you mean to me!"

They strolled in silence on the grasses surrounding the lake, as the loud twitter of birds welcomed them aboard. Their unruly fingers intertwined themselves and all those dormant woes started healing leisurely. They were around a year-and-a-half in this chasm of relationship, a stage not new enough to be broken by the distances, yet never too old to be callous about the absences. Their wandering thoughts held the reminiscences of old times, times through which they both had lived and survived. Where from they began, none of them remember anymore. They were classmates at one phase, and just acquainted strangers in another. It was at last when life arranged for a coincidental rendezvous in a crowded bus, did the sails finally catch the tide. Looking closer down, they had their own bits and pieces, very separate, very integral to the core; memories so disjoint that neither of those alone oozed the possibility of anything greater. Yet from somewhere higher up, a rising sun saw a nest-in-building atop the swamp.

They talked about things, both common and intense. The spectrum of their discussions ranged from Anuj's recent obsession for marshmallows and cheese wafers to the deepest secrets of their hearts which need a physical touch to find their voices. For Shreya, the recent expedition hadn't change Anuj at all. He was the same eccentric, impulsive dreamer who trusted in life to take its own righteous course. And in the journey, he became the one who dared to choose a course on modern art at the Academy of Fine Arts post completing his master's in physics from Presidency University - all because He believed in it. 'Perhaps he matured faster than me', she thought often while delving into the gray zones of her knowing. Back in school, during their days of Cinderella and Aladin, Anuj was almost invisible, whereas, in contrast, Shreya was the prodigal princess who shone in her crafts. Yet as life often tends to do in the end, with time it balanced their scales.

Shreya looked up at Anuj. His unmindful eyes wandered towards the distant island in the middle of the lake.

"Wish we could live there someday, all alone in our paradise", Anuj muttered to himself. Shreya smiled at the idyllic thought and pressed his fingers - some proposals don't need a verbal consent.

Word by word, phrase by phrase as Shreya's introvert soul crawled out of her cocoon, Anuj felt something was indeed amiss. In the middle of all this apparent comfort at being with each other, there was but a dark pain that's holding her captive, something too complex to match her known vocabulary, yet a feeling that shuts one out alone into the wildernesses of the desolate urban jungle. Anuj held her face into his palms, within her eyes was a glint of melancholy, a sadness of seeing a doomed kite flying down. Yet her replies gave only remote hints hidden beneath a labyrinth of riddles.

As Anuj pushed further, down the roads of companionship and the hazy slopes of its boundaries, he had this feeling that Shreya wanted herself to be understood, to seek solace and be consoled at her weak link; yet a part of her perhaps felt sorry for her own pride getting submitted - one of her elder cousins Shruti di had an abortion the day before; and as per the family rumors, her husband was not ready.

The realities of life strike hard at times; out of nowhere all of a sudden, and for Anuj that was one of those moments of hibernating senses. It was like swimming into the null of the estuary where a silent river converges into the raging seas, where the earth meets the sky, where all beliefs of good and evil go haywire.

"It's not right. No one has the right to kill off a life like that, no matter what the excuse may be", Shreya repented for no fault of hers.

He tried to defend, in his own mind, yet the steam of words he spoke were in utter disarray to the meanings he tried to convey. For a while, they both sat in silence, as of mourning a life, stillborn. Perhaps she understood, or perhaps she didn't, but she held his hands into hers and rested her head onto his shoulders, Tragedy is better at getting people closer.

The concept of creation of a nascent life from within her, the very naked notion of motherhood had always fantasized Shreya. Both had their imaginations around a family; a happy place where they could both escape together. Yet with dreams come the alien fear of a minute crack on the mirror.

Shreya's fingers brushed through the wild grasses, as the late drowning sun rose from within the tired charcoal clouds. The rains had stopped finally, and the lake seemed a lot fresher and greener. Their mischiefs kept coming back slowly as they spoke on about unrelated things, as they cracked jokes they almost forgot.

Then, with the rhythm of the flow, as their conversations moved back on the right tracks, Shreya hummed onto his ears – "If someday, you have to choose between me and our baby, what will you do?"

III

The surgery had started a few minutes back. Anuj was told to wait in the room adjacent to the OT section. There are others too – all holding their hands and closing their eyes momentarily, as if muttering silent prayers to their own gods. Fleets of doctors and nurses came out and entered the operation theatre doors, their faces all tense, their hands filled with bandages and scissors of all shapes and kinds. Anuj felt nauseous, he had always a fear towards blood, and the late afternoon catastrophe has already pushed him inches closer to his edge.

The haemophobia started from mid-school. It was the first day of their three-day stage rehearsal for annual drama competition and after a lot of debate, Anuj's team zeroed in on a musical interpretation of Macbeth. The stage was huge, and the background harp mellowed through her mellifluous notes. Anuj himself was set to play the coveted role and during the scene of the killing of King Duncan, he thrusted the sharp dagger at the pouch of viscous red fluid which was supposed to be enacted as blood. The liquid sprinkled all over in hand, as it was supposed to be, and under the hovering yellow halogen, within those few moments of shock, Anuj blacked out. The next time he woke up, within the ambient white shades of the nursing home cabin, all he felt he saw, was blood on his hands and that stinking guilt of killing a life. It took him time finally to understand it was all nothing but a creepy hallucination. Still what persisted through the ages was his apparent scare at the sight of scarlet.

Anuj sat down. The LCD monitor in front kept refreshing on loop, as the status of ongoing operations stayed the same for almost forever. The first few times (he had lost count now), Anuj's eyes foraged through the screen in search of OT-3, and every-time the status showed 'Operation in progress'. The redundancy took over slowly as the trails of incoming thought made him miss a few reloads. Yet at the breaks of subconscious, his eyes still found the same answer!

Back in those juvenile days, almost a couple decades back, when the bygone child got distressed at the twists and turns of his growing understandings, an adolescent Anuj wrote down everything in his notebook – from his first crush to the first smoke to his first masturbation. It was practically like his only friend, his only outlet for words which he couldn't express to anyone otherwise. He had this issue of stammering and that was perhaps his starting cause to not wanting to talk much. And till that reel day, when on the stage he killed King Duncan, the velvety maroon journal kept all secrets of his limited life.

Today, standing on the verge of another apocalypse, atop the falling avalanche, Anuj felt the need for his long-lost confidante. Those hard-bound sides, the ruled white pages, the dim table-lamp, the corner study table nothing is and will ever be there again as it was, yet the friend he wrote to still needed to be replied.

Anuj picked out his mobile, his routine not-so-modern version of cellphone and opened up his notes. Backed up in there, were the leads of drunken thoughts of many nights back - before life happened to happen with this meaning.

It took a while for his thumbs to move over the digital keypads in search of those new words to fill up the new blank note, to get accustomed with the process of reading one's own self, then slowly, finally the disjoint elements found their forte in unison as Anuj found words he never knew existed within.

***

"If someday, you have to choose between me and our baby, what will you do?"

That evening Shreya's question made him uncomfortable. Deep down, Anuj knew it was just an innocent query, a question asked without much thought and a one which demanded answer in the affirmative. Within the moments of his dull silences, all he tried to fathom was the intense obscurity of the question. The syllables were simple, the tone was cute, yet with the senses, they conveyed possibilities of a thousand aftermaths which Anuj felt was not the right time to think of.

"This is not a question for now Babu", his lips urged the most logical words his heart could think of. Still through the passing seconds, Shreya apprehended a latent pessimism and blunt inability in his hesitation.

"It's okay Anuj. I understand your priorities", the black kohl of her eyes looked slightly smudged and the inert thick agony in her reply reached Anuj's ears past the din & bustle of a weary city returning home. The call of an untimely Koel at the top of the nearby tree tried making amends as Anuj's heart shouted a thousand mute apologies.

"You are just not a womb to me", Anuj tried to mean his thoughts through his haphazard gestures and helpless emotional outbursts… still seldom do artists find their right words timely. Shreya's phone buzzed with a ping from Facebook. Somewhere from within the infinite web of subnet masks and network servers, someone just unknowingly challenged the somber mood of the moment with a random joke. It almost worked, the perspective of their dialogues changed as Shreya ignored any further discussion on the topic and soon smiles returned in her turbulent eyes, but

Anuj knew this was a wound under the skins and he had no option other than to trust on time to heal.

Perhaps karma awaited her chance till today. The question which Anuj thought then like a migratory seagull in late May, the season has now come for him to think this through, to mine the answer from beneath the dark crevasses of his soul.

Just one more time they spoke of this – on one intoxicated night at an unscheduled celebration on Wednesday; the midweek blues. Anuj had just received his long-awaited promotion letter and the next day was already a scheduled national holiday of some sort. The last week had been hectic for both of them and the joint causes needed to be commemorated. Anuj brought a bottle of vintage bourbon and a white Chardonnay was already at home. After dinner, they settled on the couch with the wine and The Holiday on Netflix. Anuj had a box of almonds stacked up in the top rack of kitchen especially for occasions like this and the wine tasted fine with the dry raw nuts. The intoxications took their own sweet time to get them high and when Jude Law kissed Cameron Diaz, none of them could resist getting into the arms of each other. They kissed with the smoky smell of Jim Beam on their lips and finally when he came within, there was a shy happiness in Shreya's drowsy eyes. That night, within the dim blue lights, Anuj looked into those brown pearls and said softly – "It will always be you!"

Shreya's dozy perceptions took time for the context of the words to be registered and all she said in reply was, "It's okay Anuj, you don't have to lie just because we made love".

The tunes of an instrumental raga – a midnight Basant bahar rose from somewhere in the darkness. Anuj tried explaining, but it was still not time for the injury to be fixed; some disbeliefs run too deep down the abyss to be tracked from up above the desert sands. Anuj's mind consoled his unrested conscience – "Someday, I do hope the moment not to come, but if it does, then you'll believe I am true to myself…"

Today, sitting here in this air-conditioned waiting room, a few hundred feet away from her, all that came back to him were the tiny details of those evenings they spent together, the little specifics of the nights which had stayed ignored then. The remembrances made him weak as Anuj felt the need to see her, to hold her hand or to bury his face into her palms. An Italian movie scene from years ago in his childhood came by in his arbitrary thoughts - La vita è bella. The simple love story hummed with cherry sweetness until a macabre tore the dream apart; Guido had been seized by Nazis and Dora was fighting to volunteer to be on the train. Guido held their son, Giosue, all the while staring at his Dora. Within the child's ears, he whispered the rules of the game and in her eyes were the sad tears of a separation forever. If Guido had to decide between Dora & Giosue, what would he have done?

Yes, may be the comparisons in Anuj's head had too much exaggeration. What calamity can, after all compete with a World War? Yet in his eyes, the banging glass doors of the operation theatre seemed no less sinister than the camp gates at Auschwitz.

A call came in unexpected as the dreamy trance concluded in a thud – It was the delivery boy from Urban Ladder who called to deliver their baby's new cot!

The hinges of destiny seldom get this brutally cruel and all Anuj could manage through his choking tears was – "Now in a hospital, please come back tomorrow"

Far away, on the lonely island, the lighthouse of his dreams was collapsing. He remembered all those discussions he had with Shreya, those tiny cute disagreements of how to raise their child: Martial arts or dancing, Shreya's Tintin or Anuj's Harry Potter, her school or his – all gone in an invisible mist. "There will always be a void, but I choose to share that void with you Shreya!" – Anuj typed down onto his note.

The dials of the wall-clock moved in its own perfect eternal syzygy of the sun, moon and earth and alongside those 'ticks' of time, Anuj fell in love with Shreya all over again. The girl who said a 'Yes' to his stuttering proposal a decade back had both been nurtured and eroded over the past years. The hike had changed him too, and in the quest for that vision of the future, perhaps they both lost to live in the present.

Yet, even the oyster feels the pain of getting a stone thrusted, until it grows into a pearl. This accident too may have held its own path to redemption – even cataclysms have perhaps a shiny edge…

IV

"OT-3 family member *ke achen*?" - Some hospital stuff called out from somewhere nearby.

In between, a few thousand seconds of nervous anticipation have burnt Anuj out. His forehead rested on his arms and his black-rimmed spectacles were held between the fingers of his right. The day's cycle of events had left him too tired to stay awake, but just as the call came in, his supine senses got jerked into a rough reality.

The doctor stood close to the door. He had his mask and gloves on, and Anuj, not identifying, almost walked past him.

"Mr. Sen, here"

Anuj's stature stooped a little as the doc noticed the beaded drops of sweat on his temple and two fiery desperate eyes piercing at him from within. His heart has lit up with the sudden pump of a thousand gallons of blood. So, this is the moment – on the outside, an old city is just dozing off slowly to its midnight rapid-eye sleep and inside, in this chilly cold corridor, the declaration of a death-sentence is about to be issued.

"It's time Mr. Sen. We need to select… she has lost a lot of blood internally and we are just on the verge", the doctor perhaps wanted to explain more, about the medical criticality and challenges, all the while removing the gloves of his right. But Anuj was in a hurry to answer.

"Save her, doctor. Whatever is needed, please do and save her", his voice cracked under the strain of melancholy and suppressed tears; nothing more was needed to be said. The doctor looked up at him and placed his hand on his shoulders. His fingers are warm and the humane touch gave Anuj the belief of being alive yet. Perhaps he never expected such a non-hesitant prompt reply; his years of medical experience had seen cases like this often getting hinged on the softer sides. Yet in the eyes of this man here, there is a rage that he dared not to question any further. Curtly and purposefully, like a soldier of an unfinished war, he nodded at Anuj as they parted ways.

Outside, at the pantry, the service boy was almost drooling, ready to fall off to sleep at the first given opportunity. Normally, Anuj is not someone to crave for tea. He's fond of the beverage but also very specific about the texture of the leaves and the amount of honey to be put in. Shreya on the other hand, loved her simple Red-lebel with double-toned milk and two sugar cubes.

"She doesn't like tea-bags!" - Anuj thought as he dipped his Twinning's Assam tea bag into the white milk. The guy at the counter almost didn't like the interruption and went back to his blue corner tool and placed it carefully against the corners of the wall. The color of the cup darkened slowly through shades of tortilla to fine caramel and on the first sip, the strong hint of glucose tasted too sharp for Anuj's jaded brain.

A countless ifs & buts formed and dissolved inside his mind simultaneously. The sun had started to come around for another new day and the early scavengers have declared their start of duty. From some mosque nearby, the song of a distant Ajaan came in. The rounds of tea and occasional visits to smoking zone kept delaying destiny as finally after almost six hours, the OT bulb went off.

Anuj almost stumbled upon the uneven carpets as he ran towards the doors, his heart out there hanging, beating with all the life it has as the door opened. The nurse went out without a reply, probably busier at disposing the toxic artefacts. From the narrow shafts of the open view, the doctor looked fine; there is no trace of failure on his content face as he cautiously removed his plastic dress-covers. The seeds of hope started creeping up again as Anuj earnestly waited to hear the update first-hand.

"She's okay now Mr. Sen, out of danger", the doc said in a soaring voice as he caught a sight of Anuj standing eagerly yet patiently outside the door. Somewhere, from within the coldest glaciers of the rugged tundra, a pink rhododendron blossomed its first buds. Anuj broke down almost, his eyes held tears of both love and loss; yet his gut rejoiced a win.

"You can go in, sit by her", the doc came out at last after getting changed, and while placing his spectacles on, he added with a tone of seriousness- "the doses had to be kept high, so it may take some time for her to be awake. Don't worry, she'll be okay soon".

Anuj stepped in. Inside there is a host of machines all belonging to the Matrix universe showing numerals which made no sense to his non-medical brain. And amid that entire monstrosity, there lay Shreya - the Butterfly Princess, as Anuj used to call her. She looked weak, yet her pale face had the brightness of a new born sun. She was in her checked hospital robes in the pattern of a chess board and from within the squares of black and white her breasts came up and down with her breaths; Anuj felt stranded in a tale that's beating away slowly, like hearing the sound of heart from beneath the lake of blue corals.

As he moved in slowly, his chary steps tip-toed across to the side of her bed. It's all a long wait now, a wait for her senses to come back, a wait for two eroded legos to fit in and perhaps, a wait for falling in love again at the first sight. Anuj kept looking at Shreya, her palm wrapped in his & that wait begins.

About the Authors

Sana Shanawaz

A firm believer of simplicity and spirituality, Sana Shanawaz can be found day-dreaming, observing and wandering in her flat shoes with a watch-free wrist.
The urge to speak up her thoughts has brought her closer to literature. She feels it's equally important to educate people about the injustice and prejudice which prevails in our society as it's to fight against it.

She loves all forms of literature but currently short stories is keeping her busy. Her debut short story has been selected by Ukiyoto publishing house for an anthology "Ten tales". She has tried her hand at poetry before which resulted in her poetry collection, "Love, fate and hope" available on kindle.

She spends her life balancing between her love to scribble things and attending college to study about the microbes.

Olivi Roy Chowdhury

A software engineer and a dedicated homemaker, Olivi is an introvert shy bookworm with a passion for writing. Born and brought up in the city of joy, she resides now in Kolkata. Other than books, she is an avid movie and web-series nerd and also has a passion for dancing.

Anju Chandna

Anju has spent a greater part of her working life either learning or teaching a language. She is well versed in English and German. Her love for languages prompted her to make a foray into writing. She loves to travel and writes travelogues and memoirs of her journeys. She writes short stories, articles about health and spirituality on some online forums. She got recognition for one of her blogs on 'Environment' by the jury at the prestigious Jaipur Literature Festival in 2018. Now she is a regular blogger and an aspiring fiction writer.

Abhidip Ray

Born and brought up in the city where time runs slow, the nostalgia of a romantic Calcutta genome has been the core of Abhidip Ray - the engineer turned author, an amateur musician & a social thinker. He is currently working in a multinational IT firm along with honing his long-cherished passion for writing. Introvert on the outside, Abhidip shies his life away from social media though having co-created the "As You write it" Facebook page with his childhood friend. For hobbies, Abhidip is a voracious fiction-reader, an adept movie-buff & a ninja level foodie.

His first short story "Durga in a Circus ring" has been published as part of the anthology Ten Tales by Ukiyoto.

www.ingramcontent.com/pod-product-compliance
Lightning Source LLC
LaVergne TN
LVHW041553070526
838199LV00046B/1943